W9-AAZ-286

Whatever Wanda Wanted

To Luther, Jack, and Daisy—GROUP HUG!!
and with special thanks to Shena
for her contribution to this story

First published in the United States 2002
by Phyllis Fogelman Books
An imprint of Penguin Putnam Books for Young Readers
345 Hudson Street
New York, New York 10014
Published in Great Britain 2001
by Gullane Children's Books

Printed in Belgium

1 2 3 4 5 6 7 8 9 10

Library of Congress Cataloging-in-Publication
Data available upon request

Phyllis Fogelman Books New York

WHATEVER WANDA WANTED

Jude Wisdom

Wanda's mom and dad were very busy people. So they decided that because there wasn't much time to spare, they would buy little Wanda everything she could ever want—just to show how much they cared.

The cutest doll, the coolest clothes, the prettiest kitten—Wanda only had to stamp her tiny foot and it was hers. As the years passed, the gifts grew greater. Life-sized dolls, whale-sized wading pools, theater-sized TVs—the house was stuffed with presents. Because whatever Wanda wanted, Wanda got!

At school Wanda had the biggest and best lunch box of all, but if she spotted something in someone else's box she wanted, she'd stamp and scream until she got that too.

And if one of her classmates brought in a new toy for show-and-tell, Wanda would reply, "Oh, I've got *twenty-three* of those." So, as you can imagine, the one thing Wanda didn't have was friends.

One day Wanda and her mom went shopping as usual. "I want an ice-cream cone," wailed Wanda as soon as they got there. "Certainly, darling, won't be a minute," said her mom as she rushed off to buy one.

Mr Yum yum

Wanda waited impatiently. Then, out of the corner of her eye, she spotted a store she had never seen before—and Wanda had seen *all* the stores!

As Wanda stepped inside,
she gasped in amazement.
Hanging from the ceiling were hundreds of
kites—kites of every shape and every color.
But there was one that really caught Wanda's eye.

Hanging from the ceiling was

a magnificent kite, a truly tremendous kite,

the biggest and best kite of them all!

"Can I help you?" asked the shopkeeper.
"I want that kite," snapped Wanda.
"Ah, yes—beautiful, isn't it? But that particular kite is not for sale."

"Give me the kite," hissed Wanda.

"Not for sale," said the shopkeeper.

Well, that did it. Wanda glared, Wanda stamped, Wanda spluttered, and her face turned red with fury. She ranted and raged until her eyes became as big as saucers . . .

"I WANT THAT KITE! I WANT IT NOW!" she screamed.

"ALL RIGHT!" yelled the shopkeeper.

"Take it, but beware, Wanda . . .

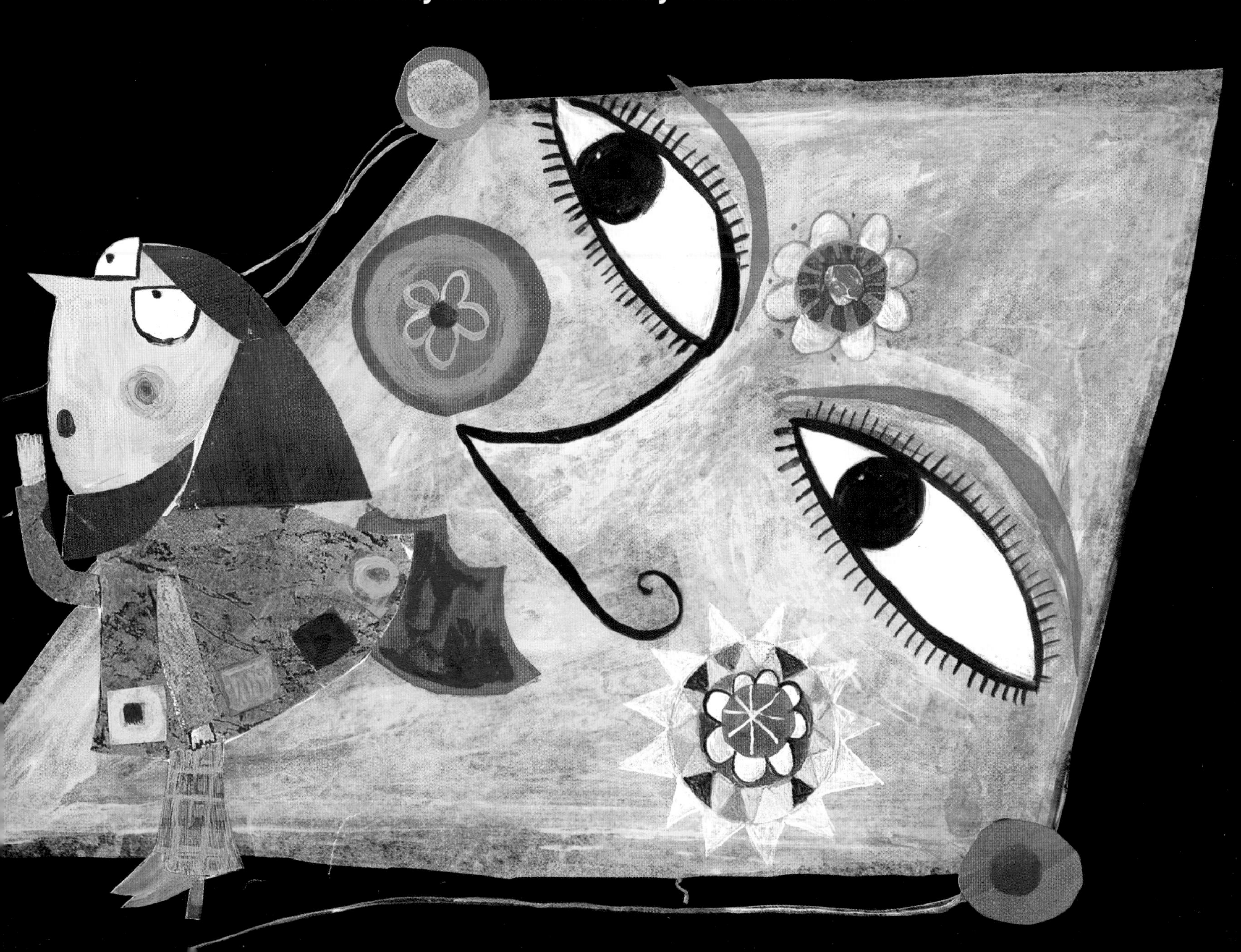

"The kite that you choose is a wonderful sight,
A marvelous, magical, mystical kite,
A truly remarkable kite, but beware,
It can do horrible things when it's up in the air!"

But Wanda wasn't listening.
She had grabbed hold of
the kite's silvery string.
"GOT YOU, KITE!" she said. . . .
"GOT YOU, WANDA!" said the kite, and before Wanda knew it,
she was being whisked through the door,
up, up, and away into the sky.

"Wanda, where are you goooooing?"
called her mom as Wanda flew past.

Wanda held on for dear life as she and the kite soared over the town. On they flew over fields and mountains and tiny villages, until they reached the ocean.

"Time you learned a few lessons," said the kite with a sharp little flick of its string, and Wanda found herself tumbling downward.

Wanda landed with a thump on a tiny desert island.
"I'm stranded," she wailed. "What am I going to do? Where are my toys and my clothes, and who will cook my breakfast, and . . ." She bit her lip and her eyes filled with tears. "THERE'S NO TV!"
Things had never looked worse for Wanda.

But as the sun warmed Wanda's face and dried her tears, she began to feel a little better. "I WILL SURVIVE!" she shouted to a surprised seagull. And that is exactly what she did.

She built a hut from bamboo sticks and made a snazzy skirt from banana leaves. She made bowls, saucepans, and spoons from coconut shells.
Then she built a fire and made some seaweed soup for lunch.

As the days went by, Wanda grew to love her new life.
One day a passing whale called Bill smelled Wanda's
delicious fish stew and decided to say hello.
Wanda invited him to stay for dinner.

Wanda and Bill soon became good friends. Every evening Bill would drop by to sample one of Wanda's wonderful meals. They talked and told jokes and looked up at the twinkling stars.

"You k[illegible] said Wanda one evening. "I don't miss my fancy clothes, or TV, or any of my toys. I just really, really, miss my mom and dad."

And a large salty tear fell from Wanda's eye and landed—plop!—in the seaweed soup.

"But, Wanda, why didn't you say so?" cried Bill.
"Hop on my back and I'll have you home in no time!"
One week later Wanda and Bill sailed into town.

Wanda's mom and dad were overjoyed to see her.

"We've searched far and wide for you!" said Dad. "We had to sell your toys, the furniture, even the house."

"And the dishwasher!" said Mom glumly.

"Don't worry," said Wanda. "I'll build us some new furniture—

Stick with me and you will see
we don't need to live like kings!
And I've decided anyway . . .

There's more to life than things!”

There's
more to
life....

~~The End~~
The Beginning!